DRAGON MASTERS

WAKING THE RAINBOW DRAGON

BY

TRACEY WEST

ILLUSTRATED BY

DAMIEN JONES

BRANCHES

SCHOLASTIC INC.

TABLE OF CONTENTS

FOR TRISTAN AND CORA,

who were chosen by the Dragon Stone. —TW

Text copyright © 2018 by Tracey West
Interior illustrations copyright © 2018 Scholastic Inc.

Library of Congress Cataloging-in-Publication Data
Names: West, Tracey, 1965- author. Jones, Damien, illustrator. West, Tracey, 1965- Dragon Masters; 10.
Title: Waking the rainbow dragon/by Tracey West; illustrated by Damien Jones.
Description: First edition. New York, NY: Branches/Scholastic Inc., 2018. Series: Dragon masters; 10
Summary: Drake has a dream about a new dragon that is somehow trapped in a cave, so Drake, Ana, and their two dragons set off to find the Rainbow Dragon's dragon master, Obi, and together they must rescue Rainbow dragon, Dayo, from Kwaku, a giant spider, who spins a deadly web.
Identifiers: LCCN 2017037057 ISBN 9781338169898 (pbk.) ISBN 9781338169904 (hardcover)
Subjects: LCSH: Dragons—Juvenile fiction. Magic—Juvenile fiction. Spiders—Juvenile fiction. Adventure stories. CYAC: Dragons—Fiction. Magic—Fiction. Spiders—Fiction. Adventure and adventurers—Fiction.
Classification: LCC PZ7.W51937 Wak 2018 DDC 813.54 [Fic]—dc23 LC record available at https://lccn.loc.gov/2017037057

13 12 11 10 9 8 7   20 21 22

Printed in China   62
First edition, July 2018
Illustrated by Damien Jones
Edited by Katie Carella
Book design by Jessica Meltzer

DRAKE'S DREAM

Drake was dreaming about a dragon.

Months before, Drake had been chosen to be a Dragon Master. He had been taken from his home and brought to King Roland's castle. There, he had learned that dragons were real.

Drake had been given his own dragon, Worm, a powerful Earth Dragon. Now they lived in the castle with the other Dragon Masters and their dragons: Kepri, a Sun Dragon; Shu, a Water Dragon; Vulcan, a Fire Dragon; and Zera, a Poison Dragon.

He had met other dragons during his adventures: Wati, a Moon Dragon; Lalo, a Lightning Dragon; Neru, a Thunder Dragon; and Frost, an Ice Dragon.

Drake dreamed about these dragons all the time. But the dragon in *this* dream was different.

She had a long body, like a snake's. Her scales shimmered with rows of stripes in different colors — red, orange, yellow, green, blue, and purple. Just like a rainbow.

It was a beautiful dream. The Rainbow Dragon flew across a blue sky. Her body curved like a rainbow. White clouds appeared and rain began to fall.

But then the rain stopped. The earth dried up. The scene changed to a dark cave. The Rainbow Dragon was curled up there. She looked frightened. A shadowy figure came toward her . . .

Drake jolted awake. His best friend, Bo, sat up across the room.

"Are you okay, Drake?" Bo asked.

"Yes," Drake replied. "I just had a dream. It felt so real. It was about a dragon."

"Are you sure it was a dream?" Bo asked. "Your Dragon Stone is glowing. Maybe Worm was trying to tell you something."

Drake looked down at the green stone that hung from a chain around his neck. Every Dragon Master wore one. It allowed them to connect with their dragons.

"You might be right, Bo!" Drake said. He jumped out of bed and quickly got dressed. "I'll find out! See you at breakfast!"

Drake ran downstairs. He raced through the underground Training Room to the caves where the dragons slept. He found Worm waiting for him.

"Worm, did you send me that dream? The dream about the Rainbow Dragon?" Drake asked.

Worm nodded. Drake's Dragon Stone glowed again. He heard Worm's voice inside his head.

Yes, Worm said. *The Rainbow Dragon needs our help!*

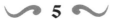

THE POWER OF RAIN

Where is the Rainbow Dragon?" Drake asked.

Worm shook his head. *I do not know.*

Drake frowned. "Griffith will know how to find her," he said.

Drake ran upstairs to the dining room. Griffith, the wizard who taught them, was there. He was eating breakfast with the other Dragon Masters who lived in the castle: Bo, Rori, Ana, and Petra.

"I told the others that Worm sent you a dream," Bo said when Drake came in.

"It was about a Rainbow Dragon," Drake explained. "Worm says she's in trouble. But that's all he knows."

Griffith nodded. "Very interesting," he said. "There is a legend about a Rainbow Dragon. She is the only one of her kind. She is very old, and very powerful. My guess is that this dragon must be sending messages to Worm somehow."

"Do you know where she lives?" Drake asked.

"I can't recall," Griffith said. "But I am sure we'll find information in one of our books. Let's get to the classroom!"

Drake wolfed down an apple, a hunk of cheese, and a piece of bread. Then the wizard and five Dragon Masters walked to the lowest level of the castle.

"What did the Rainbow Dragon look like in your dream?" Ana asked. Her dark eyes shone. "Was she beautiful?"

Drake nodded. "Yes. She had shimmering scales in rainbow colors."

"Big deal," said red-haired Rori. "What kinds of powers could a Rainbow Dragon have? Does she shoot color beams? She can't be as powerful as a Fire Dragon, like Vulcan."

"Maybe she has special powers," Petra said. "After all, Worm looks plain. But he is the most powerful dragon we know."

Rori frowned. Drake knew she couldn't argue with that. Worm could move or break things with the power of his mind. He could transport himself and others anywhere in the world in a flash.

They reached the classroom. Griffith started taking books off a shelf and handing them out.

The room was quiet as the Dragon Masters flipped through the pages.

Bo broke the silence. "I found something!" he cried. "Here is a story about a Rainbow Dragon that lives in the Kingdom of Ifri."

"Is that far from where we are, in the Kingdom of Bracken?" Petra asked.

"I know where Ifri is!" Ana said. She ran to a shelf. She came back and unrolled a map on the table.

"This is the Land of Pyramids, where I am from," she said. "And over here is the Kingdom of Ifri. It is a long way from my home, but my father has traveled there."

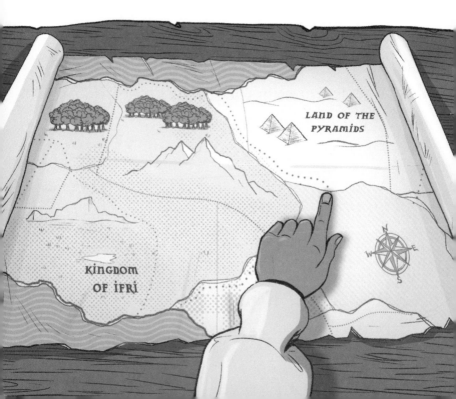

"What else does the story say?" Petra asked.

Bo read aloud, "The Rainbow Dragon has the powers of rain. Every year she comes out of her cave and brings rain to the land."

"Just like in my dream!" Drake said. "But then I saw her in her cave. She looked . . . trapped. And something was coming after her!"

"If the Rainbow Dragon is trapped, then she can't make rain," Rori said.

Ana gasped. "Oh no!" she cried. "Without rain, plants will die. There will be no food."

"I'm afraid you're right," Griffith agreed. "Ifri is in real trouble!"

A NEW DRAGON MASTER?

We've got to help the Rainbow Dragon!" Drake said. "We need to go to Ifri!"

"Ifri is very big," Ana said, pointing at the map. "How will we find the dragon?"

Drake shrugged. "Worm doesn't know where she is. So he can't transport us to her cave."

Petra looked at Griffith. "Can you use magic to find the Rainbow Dragon?"

Griffith stroked his long, white beard. "I can try."

Everyone followed the wizard to his workshop. He walked to a small table and took a cloth off a gazing ball. He bent over the glass globe and waved his hand over it.

The Dragon Masters watched the ball. A cloud of smoke swirled inside it.

Griffith frowned. "I cannot see anything," he said. "There is some kind of magic hiding the Rainbow Dragon."

Bo looked down at his Dragon Stone. "Does the Rainbow Dragon have a Dragon Master?" he asked.

"Excellent question, Bo!" Griffith said. "If we can find the Dragon Master, then maybe we can find the Rainbow Dragon."

He hurried over to a wooden box and opened it. Inside glittered a large, green stone — the Dragon Stone. Each Dragon Master's stone came from it.

"Dragon Stone, show me the Dragon Master of the Rainbow Dragon," Griffith asked.

Bright green light shot out of the stone. Moving pictures appeared inside the light.

A boy stood in front of a well. He pulled up a bucket and frowned. The well should have had water in it. But the bucket was empty. He showed it to a woman nearby.

"The well is dry," she told him. "It is like this all over Ifri."

Then the green light faded.

"Is that boy the Dragon Master?" Rori asked.

Griffith nodded. "Yes. He is the true Dragon Master chosen by the Dragon Stone," he said. "And this discovery brings us one step closer to finding the Rainbow Dragon."

The wizard clapped. "We must travel to Ifri and find this boy at once!"

A STRANGE MESSAGE

Worm can transport us to Ifri," Drake pointed out. "But how will we find the new Dragon Master once we land? The boy could be anywhere in Ifri."

"I have been working on a spell that can locate Dragon Masters," Griffith said. "I will get that ready. Drake and Ana, prepare your dragons for the journey. You two will come with me."

"Just Drake and Ana? What about the rest of us?" Rori asked.

"You must stay behind, to protect the castle," Griffith said.

Rori nodded. "Bo, Petra, and I will make sure nothing bad happens here while you're gone."

As she spoke, a sparkling blue bubble floated into Griffith's workshop.

"Look!" Petra cried.

POP! The bubble burst right in front of Griffith. A piece of paper fell into his hands. He opened it up.

"What does it say?" Ana asked.

"It is a message from the Wizard's Council," Griffith replied. Then his face went dark. "Drake, Ana, I am afraid I cannot go with you. I must deal with this message. But I trust that you will find the Rainbow Dragon. If you need help, transport back here right away."

Drake and Ana ran to the dragon caves and quickly returned to the Training Room with Worm and Kepri. Ana had put a saddle on Kepri's back.

They found Griffith looking down at the map of Ifri with Bo and Rori.

"One moment," Griffith said. "I'm putting the final spell on this map."

Griffith pointed at the map. Sparks flew from his finger.

"Map, help Drake and Ana roam. To the Dragon Master's home!" he rhymed.

The map glowed, and then it faded.

Griffith handed the map to Ana.

"This should show you the way once you land in Ifri," Griffith said. He opened a box and pulled out a Dragon Stone that dangled from a chain. He handed it to Drake. "Give this to the new Dragon Master when you see him."

Drake nodded. "Yes, Griffith." He tucked the stone into his pocket.

Petra ran up to them, out of breath.

"Wait!" she cried. She had a small bag in each hand. She gave one to Drake, and one to Ana. "I collected some food for your journey. And water."

"Thanks," Drake said, and Ana hugged Petra.

Then Ana touched Kepri with one hand, and Worm with the other. Drake touched Worm.

"Good luck!" Bo said.

"Hurry back!" Rori added.

Drake looked up at Worm. "Take us to the Land of Ifri!" he said.

Worm's body began to glow green. A bright, green light exploded in the Training Room.

Drake blinked. His body felt tingly. The green light faded, and he saw a blue sky and bright sun above his head.

"We're here!" Ana cheered.

Drake looked around. The land was very flat for as far as he could see. The tall grass was turning yellow. Some short trees popped up here and there, but their leaves were dying. There was no sign of a village.

"Which way should we go?" Drake asked.

Ana unrolled the map. A blue, glowing line appeared.

"Let's follow the magic map!" she said.

FOLLOW THE MAP

Ana and Drake walked across the grassy land. Kepri walked behind Ana, and Worm slithered behind Drake.

The hot sun shone overhead as they walked. Colorful birds flew from tree to tree.

"Most of the birds in Bracken are brown. Or gray," Drake said.

"Ifri is full of many creatures you won't find in Bracken," Ana told him.

"I hope we see more," Drake said. "But mostly, I want to find the Dragon Master!"

They walked and walked, following the map.

"My father said there are many beautiful waterfalls in Ifri," Ana remarked. "But we haven't seen any yet."

"*Everything* looks dried up," Drake said, looking at the yellow grass beneath his feet. "How much farther?"

"I don't know," she replied. "The map doesn't show where we're supposed to stop. The blue line just keeps getting longer as we walk."

Drake looked at the setting sun.

"It's getting late," he said.

"We can sleep under the stars," Ana said. "I've done it before, when I traveled with my father. Don't worry. I'll find us a good spot."

Ana soon found a spot inside a circle of trees. They both sat down in the grass.

"We'll camp here for the night," Ana said.

Drake nodded. "It feels good to rest." He opened the bag Petra had given him and took out a pouch filled with water. "And I'm so thirsty!"

He took a drink.

"Can I see the map?" Drake asked.

"Sure," Ana said. "There's just a blue dot on it now, since we've stopped."

Drake took the map from Ana. "There's got to be something here that shows us where the new Dragon Master's village is," he said. He took another sip of water — and the pouch slipped from his hand! Water spilled onto the map. The black ink faded. The blue dot disappeared.

"Drake!" Ana yelled. "What did you do?"

"It was an accident!" Drake yelled back.

"I know." Ana paused. "I'm sorry I yelled. But the spell is ruined."

Drake took a deep breath. He didn't want to fail Griffith. They had to rescue the Rainbow Dragon and save Ifri.

"Let's get some rest," he said. "We're both tired. Maybe the map will dry out overnight."

"I hope you're right," Ana said, yawning. "We'll check it in the morning."

The two Dragon Masters ate some apples and bread. The night air was chilly, so Worm curled his body around Drake. Ana snuggled against Kepri. They slept soundly.

When Drake opened his eyes, four enormous creatures surrounded their camp!

WILD FRIENDS

"Ana, wake up!" Drake yelled. "We're surrounded by dragons! Well — I *think* they're dragons!"

The four creatures were as big as dragons. But they had very long, skinny noses. They had gray, wrinkly skin instead of scales. Their big ears looked like wings to Drake.

Ana laughed. "They're not dragons, Drake," she said. "They're called elephants. And they're friendly. Well, usually they are."

Worm studied the elephants. Then his eyes began to glow. The elephants made trumpeting sounds with their trunks and shuffled their feet.

Drake's Dragon Stone glowed. He heard Worm's voice inside his head.

"Worm asked the elephants to help us. They know of a village not far from here," Drake told Ana. "They will lead us part of the way."

Ana looked down at the map. "That's a good thing, because the map still isn't working."

"Elephants to the rescue!" Drake said.

Drake and Ana ate breakfast. Then they followed the slow-moving elephants across the land. After a short time, they stopped at a shallow pool of water in the ground. The elephants sucked up the water in their long noses and then brought the water to their mouths. Worm and Kepri drank, too.

The elephants waved their trunks at Worm and walked away. Drake heard words inside his head.

The elephants told me how to get to the village. Follow me.

Drake motioned for Ana and Kepri to follow Worm.

"What about the Rainbow Dragon?" Drake asked Worm as they walked on. "Can you still feel her energy?"

It is weak, Worm replied. *Something keeps blocking my mind powers. I feel her, but her location is ... fuzzy.*

Just then, Ana cried, "Drake! Look! It's the village!"

Drake turned and saw a bunch of round houses with pointy tops. Lots of people were walking around.

Then Drake spotted the boy that the Dragon Stone had shown them.

"There he is!" Drake yelled. "It's the new Dragon Master!"

CHAPTER 7

THE CHOSEN ONE

Drake and Ana ran over to the new Dragon Master. The boy looked up at Worm and Kepri. His eyes got wide.

All the villagers began staring at the dragons. No one ran or started screaming. They actually moved closer.

"Are those . . . dragons?" the boy asked. "We have many legends about dragons here. But we have never seen any."

Drake nodded. "Yes, they are dragons," he said. "I'm Drake, and this is my dragon, Worm."

"And I'm Ana. My dragon's name is Kepri," Ana said with a smile.

"I am Obi," the boy said. "Welcome to our village. What brings you here?"

"We came to find *you*," Drake said. "You need to help the Rainbow Dragon."

Obi's mouth dropped open. The villagers all began to talk at once. A man and a woman walked up behind Obi.

"We are Obi's parents," the man said. "Please tell us where you are from, and what you know about the Rainbow Dragon."

"We came from the Kingdom of Bracken in the north," Ana replied.

Drake patted Worm's neck. "My dragon got a message from the Rainbow Dragon. She told Worm that she is in trouble."

Obi's parents looked at each other.

"This is what we have feared," Obi's father said. "The rains have not come. Water is hard to find. Plants are dying. We will soon run out of food."

"But how can Obi help?" Obi's mother asked.

"Our wizard has a Dragon Stone," Drake said. "It showed us that Obi has a special connection with the Rainbow Dragon. He is her Dragon Master. He may be the only one who can help her."

Obi shook his head. "That makes no sense," he said. "The Rainbow Dragon does not need a master. She is very powerful."

"Even the most powerful dragons need help sometimes," Ana said. "Do you know where she might be?"

Obi shook his head. "The legend says she lives in a cave somewhere," he replied. "She has never been seen. But when the rains come and a rainbow appears, we know that she has helped us."

Drake took the piece of the Dragon Stone from his pocket. "You are her Dragon Master. You can use your connection with her to help us find her."

Obi's father spoke up. "It is our good fortune that these visitors came here. You must help them, Obi."

"How can *I* help?" Obi asked. "I am just a boy. Someone else should go. A warrior. Or a healer. Or a teacher."

Ana took the Dragon Stone from Drake and put it around Obi's neck.

"The Dragon Stone picked you," she said. "You are the chosen one."

Obi looked at his parents. He looked down at the stone. Then he took a deep breath.

"All right," he said. "I will help you!"

"Yes!" Ana cheered.

"But I do not know how to find the Rainbow Dragon," Obi said.

"Worm is getting some fuzzy energy signals from the Rainbow Dragon," Drake explained. "He can lead us in the right direction."

"Then your link with the Rainbow Dragon will take us the rest of the way," Ana said. "Your Dragon Stone will glow green when you connect with her. She will lead you to her."

Obi's mother kissed her son on the head. "Be safe. The village is counting on you."

The villagers waved as Obi left with Drake, Ana, and the dragons.

THE JOURNEY

The Dragon Masters and the dragons made their way across the grassland.

"What is your kingdom like?" Obi asked as they walked.

"Well, Bracken is not flat like here," Drake replied. "There are mountains."

"And there are a lot more trees," Ana added.

"I used to live on a farm," Drake told Obi. "One year, we had a summer with very little rain. A lot of the crops died. It was scary."

Obi nodded. "Without our crops, there will be no food to eat."

Drake picked up his water pouch and frowned. "Rats. I'm almost out of water."

"Me, too," Ana added.

"I think there is a watering hole around here," Obi said. He walked ahead of Ana and Drake, looking at the ground. Then he broke away from the path.

"Where are you going?" Drake asked. He and Ana hurried to catch up to Obi.

"These are animal tracks," Obi explained, pointing to the ground. "And they lead right . . . here."

He pushed through some bushes, and they stepped into a clearing. A small pool of water bubbled up from the dirt.

"Wow!" Drake cried.

"You found water!" Ana said happily.

They filled their pouches with water. Worm took a drink, too.

Then Obi led them back through the bushes.

Suddenly, Obi froze. He stopped Drake with his arm.

A strange animal stood in the grass ahead of them. It looked like a very big, very hairy pig with long, white tusks!

The animal's ears twitched. Then it turned around and locked eyes with Drake.

KWAKU!

Obi put a finger to his lips. "*Shh!* Don't move," he whispered to Drake and Ana. "It's a warthog! If you make any fast movements, it might attack."

Obi raised his arms above his head and crept up to the warthog. Then he made a very loud, scary noise.

ROOOAAAAAR!

Frightened, the warthog squealed and scrambled away.

"Wow, Obi! That was awesome!" Drake said. "You sounded like a big, scary cat."

"I was pretending to be a lion," Obi said. "Do you have lions in Bracken?"

Drake shook his head.

"They are big, fierce cats," Obi explained.

Ana smiled at Obi. "You are very smart and brave. I think you were born to be a Dragon Master."

"Yes," Drake agreed. "You found water for us. You scared away the warty hog. You're amazing!"

Obi gave them both a shy smile. They caught up to Worm and Kepri, who had started moving again.

A few minutes later, Obi's Dragon Stone began to glow faintly.

"Obi, look!" Drake cried, pointing. "Your stone is glowing. The Rainbow Dragon is trying to connect with you."

Worm stopped.

Obi must lead us the rest of the way, he told Drake. *His connection is stronger than mine.*

"Worm says you should lead us," Drake told Obi.

"How do I do that?" Obi asked.

"Can you feel the pull of your dragon's energy?" Ana said.

Obi closed his eyes. "It's weak, but I can feel it!" he said, his voice rising with excitement. "It's like . . . she's in my head."

"Great! Now walk toward that energy," Ana instructed.

Obi started walking. They followed him to a low hill. A big hole in the hill led to an underground tunnel.

Obi gazed into the tunnel. "I . . . I think she is in here," he said.

Ana looked up at Kepri. "Can you please light the way for us?"

A white ball of light floated out of Kepri's mouth. It hung in the air, lighting up the dark tunnel.

The ball floated down the tunnel, and the others followed it.

They went a short way and then stopped.
A thick spiderweb blocked the entrance to a
cave!

"Whoa! A *very* big spider must have made
this," Drake said.

Obi gasped. "Kwaku!" he cried.

"What's a kwaku?" Drake asked.

"Kwaku is a giant spider that my people tell stories about," Obi explained. "Sometimes he is a hero. Sometimes he makes trouble."

"Are they true stories?" Drake asked.

"I thought they were just legends," Obi said. "But look at this web! Only Kwaku could have spun it."

Suddenly, Drake's Dragon Stone began to glow. He heard Worm's voice inside his head.

Obi is right. Kwaku has trapped the Rainbow Dragon inside her cave!

STUCK IN A WEB

rake ran to the giant web blocking the entrance to the cave. He started pulling on the strands.

"I can't break the web!" he said. "It is too strong and sticky!"

"Drake, stop!" Ana said. "If there is a giant spider behind there, we need a plan."

She turned to Obi. "In the stories about Kwaku, how is he defeated?" she asked.

"I don't think he has ever been beaten. Kwaku is a magical trickster. He usually uses tricks to escape," Obi said.

"There must be a way to stop him," Drake said.

"Well, some stories say he works for the ruler of the sun. So maybe the sun can stop Kwaku?" Obi guessed.

"Hmm," Ana said. "Kepri might not be the ruler of the sun. But she has the powers of the sun! Maybe she can break through the web and fight Kwaku's magic."

Ana turned to Kepri. "Use a sunbeam on the web!"

Kepri opened her mouth and shot a strong beam of sunlight at the thick spiderweb. The strands of the web began to shimmer. Then they disappeared!

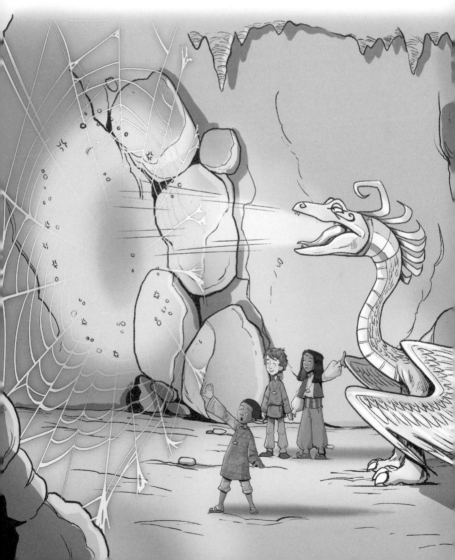

"It worked!" Drake cried.

Obi put a finger to his lips. "Quiet."

They stepped into the cave. The ball of white sunlight still floated in the air, lighting the dark space.

Drake and Ana gasped.

A dragon with a very long body was wrapped in a cocoon of spider silk. Through the silk, Drake could see the dragon's rainbow-colored scales.

"The Rainbow Dragon!" Obi cried.

"Kepri, use another sunbeam to get rid of the cocoon!" Ana commanded.

The Sun Dragon aimed a strong beam of sunlight at the Rainbow Dragon. The webs began to shimmer, but before they could disappear...

Click, click, click! A loud, clicking sound began to echo through the cave. Kepri stopped shooting her sunbeam and turned toward the sound.

A giant spider crawled out of the shadows! His eight long legs were black with yellow stripes. His round body had a black-and-yellow pattern. Eight round, black eyes stared at the Dragon Masters and their dragons. Drake, Ana, and Obi started to slowly back up.

Eeeeeeee! With a cry, the spider scurried toward them. Kepri and Worm charged forward, protecting the Dragon Masters.

"Kepri, hit him with sunlight!" Ana yelled.

Kepri aimed a beam of sunlight at Kwaku. The spider jumped up to avoid it. He hung upside down from the ceiling of the cave.

In a flash, he shot webs at Kepri.

The webs wrapped around her mouth. Kepri couldn't fight back. The webs magically grew and twisted all around Kepri's body.

"Kepri!" Ana cried.

Worm's body began to glow green. But before he could use his powers, Kwaku hit him with webs, too. The webs wrapped around Worm. Within seconds, he was trapped inside a cocoon.

"Quick, hide!" Drake yelled to Ana and Obi. "We can't help the dragons if Kwaku gets us, too!"

The friends raced behind a big rock. Drake touched his Dragon Stone.

"Worm, can you hear me?" he whispered.

Drake's Dragon Stone glowed faintly. Drake heard a muffled voice in his head.

He turned to Ana and Obi. "Worm is trying to tell me something, but I can't understand him," he said. "The cocoon must be blocking Worm's powers!"

"I can't hear Kepri's voice in my head, either," Ana whispered.

"What now?" Drake asked. "We can't fight Kwaku without our dragons!"

A STRONG CONNECTION

Drake, Ana, and Obi stayed hidden behind the rock. But the clicking sound of the giant spider grew louder as he got closer.

Click, click, click.

"We should go get help," Obi whispered.

"Who will help us?" Drake asked.

Click, click, click.

"We can't stay here," Ana said. "Kwaku is going to trap us in cocoons, too!"

Obi stood up. His Dragon Stone was glowing.

"Obi, get down!" Drake hissed.

Obi didn't listen to Drake. He stared at the Rainbow Dragon.

Kwaku spotted Obi with one of his eight eyes.

"Watch out, Obi! Kwaku will hit you with one of his webs!" Drake yelled.

Obi didn't run. He talked to the Rainbow Dragon.

"Our village needs you," he said. "Please help us."

Then Obi's Dragon Stone began to glow brighter ... and brighter ... and brighter!

"Whoa!" Drake told Ana. "I've never seen a Dragon Stone glow like that before. It's even brighter than Worm when he uses his powers!"

The bright green light filled the cave. The Dragon Masters had to shield their eyes.

Eeeeeeeeeeeeeeee! Kwaku shrieked.

As the powerful light grew, he skittered deep into the cave.

The light faded. Drake looked around. The cocoons around the dragons were shimmering, just like when Kepri's sunlight hit the giant web.

The cocoons disappeared. Drake and Ana ran to their dragons.

Ana patted Kepri's head.

"Worm! Are you okay?" Drake asked.

I am fine, Worm replied.

Drake smiled and glanced over at Obi.

The new Dragon Master was standing next to the Rainbow Dragon. She was free of the cocoon, and hovering above the floor.

"She's so beautiful," Ana whispered.

The Rainbow Dragon's colorful scales shimmered in the dim light of the cave. She had a long, snakelike body like Worm's. She did not have wings.

Obi turned to Drake and Ana. "She says it's time to make it rain. And she wants me to go with her."

Drake nodded.

Obi climbed onto the Rainbow Dragon's back. Then they floated out of the cave, past Drake, Ana, and their dragons.

Ana nudged Drake. "Let's go!"

They ran outside, followed by Worm and Kepri. The sun shone brightly in the blue sky.

The Rainbow Dragon flew up, up above the grassy lands, with Obi on her back.

"I'll meet you back at the village!" Obi called down.

Obi and the dragon flew higher and higher.
Gray clouds appeared in the sky.

Then Drake felt one cold, wet drop on his cheek.

"Rain!" he cheered.

DRAGONS IN THE SKY

More clouds filled the sky. The rain began to fall harder.

"Obi will be busy for a while," Drake said. "Let's go tell his parents what happened."

Ana nodded. She touched Kepri with one hand and Worm with the other.

Worm transported them to the village in a flash of green light. They found the villagers standing outside in the rain.

Obi's parents ran up to them.

"Where is Obi?" Obi's mother asked.

"He is safe!" Drake replied. "Kwaku the spider was keeping the Rainbow Dragon prisoner. Obi freed her. They are both up in the sky now, making rain."

Obi's mother took Ana by the hand. "Come, both of you. I think this will be a long rain. Step inside our hut, where it is warm and dry."

Obi's mother fed them bowls of hot stew.

Just as they were finishing, a shout came from outside the hut.

"Look!"

Drake, Ana, and Obi's parents rushed outside.

The clouds were floating away. The sun was shining. The sky was bright blue. And the Rainbow Dragon was floating in the sky. Her body curved, just like a rainbow. Her colorful scales shimmered brightly. Obi sat on her back, beaming happily.

Everyone stared at the sight, amazed.

Then Ana's Dragon Stone began to glow. She smiled.

"Kepri wants to fly, too," she said.

Ana climbed onto Kepri's back. Kepri flew up into the sky. Misty waterdrops filled the air. She shot a beam of sunlight from her mouth. The light hit the water droplets and made a rainbow right underneath the Rainbow Dragon.

Drake grinned. "It's a double rainbow!"

DAYO'S STORY

Kepri and the Rainbow Dragon flew down from the sky. Obi slid off the Rainbow Dragon's back and ran to his parents.

"Mom! Dad!" he cried.

"Hooray for Obi!" the villagers cheered.

Obi's Dragon Stone began to glow.

"The Rainbow Dragon wants me to tell you her story," he said. "Her name is Dayo."

"Dayo," Ana repeated, hopping off Kepri. "That's a cool name!"

"Did she say how Kwaku trapped her in her cave?" Drake asked.

"Kwaku tricked her," Obi went on. "He told the Rainbow Dragon he knew the most beautiful song in the world. She asked to hear it. But the song was really a spell that made her fall asleep. Then he spun a cocoon around her."

Some of the villagers gasped.

"Why would he do that?" Ana asked.

"Kwaku was mad at Dayo," Obi explained. "The last time the rains came, water flooded his den. He trapped Dayo because he didn't want that to happen ever again."

Obi's father nodded. "He is a tricky one!" he said.

"Dayo couldn't move, but her mind was still powerful," Obi continued. "She called out for help. And Drake's dragon, Worm, heard her."

Drake patted Worm. "And then Worm told me," he said. "And then we found Obi."

"Dayo is grateful to you both, and your dragons," Obi told Drake and Ana.

Two young boys ran into the village.

"The waterfall is flowing again!" one of them shouted.

The villagers cheered and hugged one another.

"I'm glad the Rainbow Dragon is safe now," Ana said. "But what if Kwaku tries to trick her again?"

"Dayo says she knows not to trust Kwaku ever again," Obi replied. "And now that she and I have connected, she will call on me if she is in trouble."

Obi looked down at his glowing Dragon Stone. A sad look crossed his face.

"Dayo says that she must go back to her cave," he said. "She must watch over the land, like she always has."

He hugged his dragon. "I will miss you, Dayo," he said.

The Rainbow Dragon wrapped her body around Obi, giving him a quick hug.

Then she floated up into the sky and flew away.

"I was hoping that you and Dayo could come back to Bracken and train with us," Drake said.

"We cannot, but thank you," Obi said. "The Rainbow Dragon belongs in this land. And so do I."

"I understand," Drake replied.

Obi's father stepped forward. "Thank you for helping our village," he said. "You will always be welcome here."

"Thank you," Drake said. "Now we must get home. Our friends will be getting worried about us."

"Good-bye!" Ana called out.

Drake and Ana touched their dragons. Then Worm transported the four of them back to Bracken in a flash of green light.

TROUBLE AT THE CASTLE

Diego, what are you doing?!"

The first thing Drake and Ana heard when they landed in the Training Room was Griffith's voice. He sounded angry. They quickly left Worm and Kepri and followed the sound to the classroom.

"Please stop!" Griffith was yelling at a short, round wizard. Diego was Griffith's friend, and he had helped the Dragon Masters many times. But now he was making a mess of the classroom. He took book after book off the shelf and tossed each one on the floor.

"Where is it? It has got to be here!" Diego muttered to himself. He ignored Griffith.

"Diego, calm down!" Griffith ordered.

Suddenly Diego held up a book. "I found it!" he cried. He spun around, facing Griffith.

Griffith gasped. His mouth dropped open in surprise.

That's when Drake noticed something — Diego's eyes were red!

"Diego! Let us help you!" Drake cried, but Diego had a special talent. He could transport, just like Worm.

Poof! The wizard disappeared.

Rori, Bo, and Petra came running into the classroom.

"What's all the yelling about?" Rori asked. Then she stopped. "Drake! Ana! You're back!"

"Yes, and we saved the Rainbow Dragon," Ana said. "But that's not why Griffith was yelling. Diego was just here!"

"His eyes were red—the color of Maldred's dark magic," Drake said. "I think he was under a spell!"

Everyone was quiet. Maldred was an evil wizard. He had attacked King Roland's castle and tried to take the dragons away. The Dragon Masters, Griffith, and Diego had stopped him.

Bo turned to Griffith. "But you and Diego sent Maldred to the Wizard's Council Prison," he said. "He can't use magic while he's in there."

"That is what the council warned me about earlier..." the wizard replied. "Maldred has escaped."

"No!" Rori yelled. She balled her hands into fists. "We need to find him!"

"What would he want with Diego?" Petra asked.

"It looks like Maldred has used Diego to steal a book from me," Griffith said as he riffled through the bookshelf. "But — no, wait, it couldn't be . . ." His face turned pale. "Diego took my book about the Naga, a dragon of legend."

"Is that bad?" Drake asked.

Griffith nodded. "Very bad. If Maldred is seeking the Naga, then the whole world is in danger!"

TRACEY WEST was once lucky enough to see a double rainbow, and she hopes you'll get to see one, too.

Tracey has written dozens of books for kids. She writes in the house she shares with her husband, her three stepkids (when they're home from college), and her animal friends. She has three dogs and one cat, who sits on her desk when she writes! Thankfully, the cat does not weigh as much as a dragon.

DAMIEN JONES lives with his wife and son in Cornwall — the home of the legend of King Arthur. Cornwall even has its very own castle! On clear days you can see for miles from the top of the castle, making it the perfect lookout for dragons.

Damien has illustrated children's books. He has also animated films and television programs. He works in a studio surrounded by figures of mystical characters that keep an eye on him as he draws.

DRAGON MASTERS
WAKING THE RAINBOW DRAGON

Questions and Activities

Drake has a dream at the beginning of the story. Who sends him the dream? Why?

Why is the Rainbow Dragon important to the Kingdom of Ifri? Turn back to pages 11 and 36.

How did Kwaku trick the Rainbow Dragon? (Hint! Look back on page 79.)

At the end of the story, the Dragon Masters discover that Diego is under Maldred's spell. What do you think the dark wizard wants with Diego? Predict what will happen in the next book. Write your own beginning chapter, and draw your own action-packed pictures.

Drake and Ana see elephants and a warthog in the Kingdom of Ifri. What wild animal would you most like to see in real life? Where does this animal live? Using nonfiction books and the Internet, learn more about this animal.